Chye Chye Skudigus

By Esther Sellars

Copyright 2022 Esther Sellars

Celticfrog Publishing

Clearwater, BC

ISBN 978-1-989092-70-5

The afternoon sun was beating down on the field. Walter
stopped hoeing the never ending weeds in the long row of turnips.
He pulled out his hanky to wipe his brow, glancing around he
could see his brothers Frank and Felix were still working with
his sisters Grace and Wilhelmina,pulling mustard weed from
the potato patch. They usually worked together but his mother
caught him fooling around and separated him from the others.
It was Frank that had started the horse play but as usual it
was Walter that had been caught. Walter did not like weeding
but as his mother had explained,so many times it was necessary
in order for the garden to grow enough food to keep them
through the long hard winter. He started hoeing again and
tried to keep in mind the evenings for they made up for the
long hard days.

Each evening after they had washed up supper would be cooked
on a big old stove out behind the house. The stove had been
moved out back in the early spring as it was too hot to cook
in the house during the warmer months. Each evening after the
meal was over they would light a camp fire to keep the mosquitos
away and best of all each night his mother would tell them a
story.He smiled to himself as he remembered the night before.
By the time they had settled around the fire the stars were
twinkling brightly in the sky. Wilhelmina had been gazing
at them in wonder when she asked momma how they got there.
"Well" said momma as we all gathered around her as we knew
a story was about to be told.

"WELL" she said, drawing a long breath, "Many, many years ago
there was a small town in the Cariboo, nestled in between two
rivers and a high bluff, where the people lived a very peaceful
and plentiful life.
The town consisted of a General Store, a stable, the school,
the Barber shop, and the Church with its high steeple. The
Church also served as a meeting place for the town fathers
once a week. Oh yes and the Hotel, It was the towns newest
building, There were about a dozen homes right in town, each
with their neat white picket fences around the neatly kept
yards, and there was at least twice as many families that lived
on farms nestled in the surrounding hills. Just north of the
town on the top of the bluff, there was a very large Indian
Village.

This small community had never known anything but good times
for their crops never failed and everyone got along with
each other. The only time they came close to disagreeing was
when they were trying to decide where they were going to build
the hotel. Mrs Johnson was going to be the cook and she wanted
the Hotel at her end of the town, Mr. Andrews who had the Barber
Shop wanted it close to him, but in the end the Hotel was built
close to the stables where the horses from the stage were
cared for and fed.
One stormy afternoon their world changed, for along with a
summer's storm, came a stranger.
Little Alex had been chasing a rabbit with his dog Trapper
when he heard a voice that made chills run up and down his
spine.

He quickly grabbed Trapper and hid in the bushes. He lay
trembling as the gruff voice came closer. He peeked through
the bush and he saw the strangest looking man coming along the
path swinging a large double axe to and fro, his hair was so
long it almost reached the ground, his beard was tangled in
his hair and almost as long, his clothes were made from the
hides of animals. His gruff voice rumbled and as he came
closer Alex could hear him say to the small frightened animals
that scattered out of his way..."Keep out of the way of my
axe or you'll not live to see the morning light for my name
is Chye Chye Skudigus and I destroy everything in my path."
Alex watched in horrer as some of the little animals were not
fast enough to get away. He waited until Chye Chye Skudigus
went around the next bend in the path, calling his dog to
follow him, he raced down the side of the hill on his secret
short cut to town. He knew he had to run fast in order to
warn the towns people, he hoped that they would believe him.

His side ached and his breath was coming in short gasps as he
burst through the door of his house. His Mother had been
kneading dough to make bread for supper, She quickly wiped
the flour from her hands and ran across the room to her son.
He told his mother what he had seen. His mother became
pale, she grabbed her son by the hand and said they had better
get over to the Church as there was a meeting and all of the
men would be there.

Everyone turned around when the doors of the Church burst
open. Alex ran to his father as his mother told the group
what her son had told her. They knew that they had to act
fast as Chye Chye Skudigus would be entering their town any
moment now. Not having time to plan anything the group raced
to the edge of town where the path entered town, much to
their horror Chye Chye Skudigus was just entering the main
street.

He was bent forward walking into the wind swinging his axe,
when he spotted the group blocking his way he growled at them
"keep out of the way of my axe fools or you"ll not see the
morning light or my names not Chye Chye Skudigus" and he started
swinging his axe to and fro. The men scattered as Chye Chye
Skudigus continued on. The Mayor gasped in pain as he was not
quick enough and the axe caught him in the shoulder. Mr Andrews
was the first to reach Mayor Harpers side, he called to the
others to come and help him carry the Mayor over to old Doc
Bakers. Once they had reached the Doc's house they decided the
first thing they had to do was warn the rest of the people
both in the town and the farms surrounding the town. They left
the Mayor with the Doc and hurried off to warn everyone before
any one else could get hurt. They agreed to meet at the Church
once everyone had been warned.

Doc Baker quickly put neat stitches in the Mayors shoulder
and helped him home for there would be no meeting for the
Mayor tonight as he was in too much pain. He then went door
to door to all the houses in town for he had been assigned
to warn the women left in town as their husbands rode from farm
to farm to warn them of Chye Chye Skudigus.
It was late that night before the last of the men walked through
the heavy doors of the Church. It was to be the first of many
meetings to come in the next few months. Chye Chye Skudigus
continued to keep the people hiding in fear everytime he
passed their way, taking what he wanted and destroying anything
blocking his way. It seemed that Chye Chye Skudigus had decided
to settle in their town. Finally late one night as the men
sat in a huddle at the Church with the doors bolted shut
Billy Keen the store keeper stood up and said "I think that
it is time that we turn to Chief Many Fingers for help. I
am sure that he could get his medicine man to help us."

The men looked at each other with the first glimmer of hope
that they had for some time. The Mayor stood up and lit
his pipe thoughtfully. "That is the best idea that anyone has
come up with yet. I think we should meet in the morning
and go to the Bluff and ask him"
"Perhaps it would be a good idea to bring some gifts for the
Chief and his people," suggested Thomas Hoye the Hotel
Keeper.
"That is an excellent idea," replied Zed, who ran the stables,
"I have a pair of Clydesdales I'm sure the Chief would like."
They all agreed that they would meet early in the morning as
Chye Chye Skudigus never got up until the sun was setting. For
the next hour the men decided what each one would bring,
and then they separated, heading for home, for they knew
their families would be just as excited when they heard that
the men finally had a plan to rid themselves of Chye Chye
Skudigus.

The Mayor was the first to arrive carrying a large gold key
that was to be a symbol to show that the Indians were welcome
in their town and that they would be welcome in the planning
of the town. Shortly after he arrived Zed, who owned the stable
showed up leading a matched pair of clydesdales, their manes
braided with red ribbons. They pranced knowing that they were
part of a very important event. Jim Andrews was close behind
he carried his finest razor, He knew the Chief did not shave
but was sure that he would find good use of such a sharp blade.
Next was Billy Keen, the store Keeper, He had a hard time in
choosing his gift. At first he thought maybe the barrel of juicy
red apples that were in the corner of the store, and then
the 100 pound bag of flour that had a brightly painted picture
of Robin Hood on the side of it, but as he walked over
to pick it up he spotted the bolt of red checkered cloth that
had arrived on the last stage, It was for Mrs. Johnson, she
was going to make table clothes and curtains for the restaurant
with it. She would be disappointed but he knew she would

understand for the welfare of the community was more important
than curtains and table clothes.
Then came Mrs. Campbell carrying a rather large basket of freshly
baked bread, pies and sugar cookies. Everyone in the valley
knew that she was the best cook for many a mile. Ronnie was
hanging on her skirt running to keep up. He was too young and
full of mischief to be left alone. The last time his mother had
left him in the house by himself, while she ran out to the well
for a bucket of water, he had tried to make the old black cat
white with the bag of flour. What a mess, it had taken her
all morning to get the house back to normal.
Dr Baker was the last to arrive with his buggy loaded down
from the rest of the towns people. There was everything one
could imagine from four laying hens to a hand stitched quilt
that the womens club had made last winter.

Satisfied that everyone was present and accounted for, they
loaded the rest of the gifts in Doc Bakers buggy and began
the long walk up the hill to the top of the bluff. Ronnie
sat in the buggy between his mother and Doc Baker, it wasn't
long before the rocking of the buggy put him to sleep. His
mother let out a sigh of relief, the trip would be quiet as
long as Ronnie slept for he chattered constantly rarely
stopping long enough to hear the answer of his never ending
questions.
It was a beautiful morning, the dew still on the grass, the
birds were chirping as the fox crossed the road going home
after a night of hunting.
They were filled with a feeling that none of them had felt
for a long time...Hope.

As they entered the village Chief Many Fingers was just returning
from his morning hunt. The Spirits had smiled upon him this
morning and he had brought back enough game to last his people
the rest of the week.
The Mayor wasted no time in telling the Chief the reason for
their visit and the gifts. Chief Many Fingers, who by the
way,was so named because he was born with six fingers on each
hand, listened patiently nodding now and then to acknowledge
what was being said.He understood the fear that the towns people
felt, for only last week his people had felt the fury of Chye
Chye Skudigus. He accepted the gifts and said that he would
talk with his Medicine Men immediately. Foolish people he
thought to himself as he watched them leave, there was no need
for gifts but seeing it was so important to them he accepted,
He stood for a moment to admire the horses. He did not linger
for too long as he had to prepare for his next guests.

Shortly after the sun was high in the sky when the Chiefs guests
began to arrive. Coming out of the forest were the Elders
and Medicine Men from all of the neighboring tribes. Chief
Many Fingers had been wise enough from the start to realize
that he would need all the help he could get to rid the world
of someone as evil as Chye Chye Skudigus.
He greeted each man as he entered the camp, they would eat
and visit among the fires of the camp for it had been many
moons since they all sat in the same camp. Once this was done
they would sit forming a circle around the main camp fire and
get down to the business at hand. Chief Many Fingers looked
at the group of men and let out a sigh of relief, for he knew
that along with the power of healing they also had the knowledge
of Black Magic that would be needed to complete this task.

Finally everyone had eaten and the talk had come to a halt.
Chief Many Fingers led the men to the fire to sit and smoke
the pipe while a solution was sought. He told them of Chye
Chye Skudigus and the path of sorrow that he left.
He paused looking into each face that circled the fire, each man
was deep in thought as they knew that they were facing the most
difficult task that any of them had ever encountered. They
admired the wisdom of Chief Many Fingers for they realized
that in order to rid the world of Chye Chye Skudigus that they
would have to unite their powers for that alone they did not
have the strength but united, they would prove to be stronger.
Lone Butt, the youngest of the bunch, blurted out that they could
change him into a rain cloud. Blue River looked thoughtful
as he shook his head saying that there was a possibility that
he could return to earth without anyone knowing until much
distruction had taken place and he would be free to roam the
earth causing sorrow and pain once again.

It was agreed that whatever they did to Chye Chye Skudigus it
would have to be done in such a manner that they would be able
to tell at a glance from anywhere in the world that he was
still under the spell of the Medicine Men and the world was safe
from him.
The eldest of the Elders, who had been sitting quietly listening
to the others stood and spoke. "Many many moons ago when I
was a young hunter my Grandfather told me of a spell that would
be needed in the days when my sight dimmed from age. I believe
the time has come. He told me there would be a gathering of
many Elders and Medicine Men and that with the power and wisdom
of these men and the secret potions of all along with two fingers
of one that has more, a solution would be found." Chief Many
Fingers looked at his hands, "So be it " he said.

They still had to figure out where they would send Chye Chye
Skudigus, after many ideas Chief Many Fingers stood and said
"I think I have the solution, We have the sun to brighten our
sky in the day and only the moon at night, I think that if we
sent Chye Chye Skudigus to the moon and cast a spell on him
so that every night he would sharpen his axe and the sparks
could fly through the sky to bring more light to the earth
we could tell for any where on earth that he was where he belongs,
We could call the sparks stars."
So it came to pass that Chye Chye Skudigus was to spend the rest
of eternity on the moon sharpening his axe.   On a cold winters
night when the north wind is still if you listen real hard
you can hear his raspy voice chanting "Chye Chye Skudigus is my
name and if you want to see the morn light you had better
stay clear of my axe."

"And that my children is how the stars got to be in the sky."
said momma. "Now off to bed with all of you as we have much
work to do in the morning." "Yes,"thought Walter,as he helped
his mother put the fire out,the work will be hard but along
with it we will be told another story.

9 781989 092705